TWiLiGHt's SPaRKLY SLeePoVeR SURPRiSe

by Perdita Finn

Little, Brown and Company
New York ✳ Boston

HASBRO and its logo, MY LITTLE PONY, EQUESTRIA GIRLS and all related characters are trademarks of Hasbro and are used with permission. © 2016 Hasbro. All Rights Reserved.

Little, Brown and Company

Hachette Book Group
1290 Avenue of the Americas, New York, NY 10104
Visit us at lb-kids.com

Little, Brown and Company is a division of Hachette Book Group, Inc.
The Little, Brown name and logo are trademarks of Hachette Book Group, Inc.

The publisher is not responsible for websites (or their content) that are not owned by the publisher.

First Edition: May 2016

Library of Congress Control Number: 2016933832

ISBN 978-0-316-26699-4

10 9 8 7 6 5 4 3 2 1

RRD-C

Printed in the United States of America

For Sophie, Katie, Edith, Seraphina, and Nickie—in memory of many a sleepover

CONTENTS

* * *

PROLOGUE

Mirror, Mirror on the Wall

★ ★ ★

Twilight Sparkle couldn't believe what she was seeing. One minute, she was enjoying a picnic with some girls at Canterlot High, and the very next, there was a sudden blast of light from the Wondercolt statue. Twilight Sparkle blinked at the girl who appeared.

She looked totally like her. Twilight Sparkle was looking at her exact double.

This girl had the same violet hair with pink streaks. She had the same round brown-purple eyes with long, dark lashes. She was even wearing the same plum skirt, blue blouse, and purple boots. It was like looking in a mirror, except this other girl wasn't wearing glasses.

Who was she?

"I'm sorry I didn't get here sooner!" the girl explained breathlessly. "I didn't get your messages until just now because I was caught in this time-travel loop, and honestly, it was *the* strangest thing that has ever happened to me...." The girl's mouth dropped open. She stared at Twilight Sparkle. "Make that the second strangest." She gulped.

Confused, Twilight Sparkle gave the girl an awkward wave. The girls behind her burst out laughing.

"Well, I'll be." Applejack grinned. "Twilight Sparkle, meet Twilight Sparkle."

"Princess Twilight Sparkle from Equestria, meet Twilight Sparkle, the new girl who just transferred to Canterlot High from Crystal Prep," explained Sunset Shimmer helpfully.

Pinkie Pie giggled and tossed her curly, pink locks. "Twilight—I mean, Princess Twilight—the new Twilight—I mean, the new girl—came to Canterlot High during the Friendship Games. She opened up a portal while investigating magic. Everyone nearly disappeared into it. Almost, but just in time, Sunset Shimmer helped Twilight Sparkle—the new Twilight—recover because she remembered what it was like to turn into a she-demon by accident and all the power in the world can't teach you about friendship and..." Pinkie Pie paused to catch her breath. "And...well...Twilight— never-been-a-pony Twilight—what you need to know is that Princess Twilight Sparkle knows *everything* about friendship."

"*Everything?*" asked Twilight Sparkle, amazed.

"Everything," agreed all the Equestria Girls together.

"That's not true!" protested Princess Twilight. "Every time I make a new friend, I learn something new about friendship. Every friendship is special. Every friendship is different. It's nice to meet you, Twilight Sparkle! I guess I always knew I had my double in your world, but it's wonderful to see you in person!" She smiled. "I like your boots!"

Twilight Sparkle blushed. "It's nice to meet you, too," she said shyly. "But how come we look alike?"

How could the girls explain it?

"There's a world of magic—" began Rarity.

"That's the world you tapped into during the Friendship Games," Rainbow Dash interrupted.

"And everyone there is a pony, and each of us has a pony who shares our name and looks exactly like us, or only really looks like us when they come to our world like Sunset Shimmer and Princess Twilight did, only we've never met our pony pairs before. This is the first time for any of us," gushed Pinkie Pie.

"That's about right." Applejack nodded.

"Oh," said Twilight Sparkle. She was overwhelmed. How could she have a double who was the Princess of Friendship? Until she came to Canterlot High from Crystal Prep, she'd never even had one single friend. Not one. Except for her dog, Spike. She patted him on the head.

"Spike!" said Princess Twilight.

Spike looked back and forth between the two girls and rubbed his eyes with his paw.

"How do you know Spike?" asked Twilight Sparkle.

"I have a little dragon called Spike. He looks like a dog in this world," said Princess Twilight. "But he can talk."

"Me too!" barked Spike. "But I've never been a dragon."

All the girls laughed. There was so much to catch up on. The girls talked at once as they told Princess Twilight about the Friendship Games. Everyone had been so mixed up when they had first met Twilight Sparkle from Crystal Prep. They had thought she was the Princess of Friendship who had gone to Canterlot High once upon a time.

"Especially Flash Sentry," said Rarity.

"What's he going to do when he sees two of you?" Pinkie Pie wondered.

Princess Twilight's face fell. "Oh, but he won't. I can't stay very long. Besides it looks like you've solved all your problems with the portal you wrote me about."

"We have," said Rainbow Dash. "Still, we always have lots to learn about friendship. You have your own Twilight Sparkle now, and I've got a feeling that she knows a lot about friendship."

Princess Twilight smiled.

The girls beamed happily at their new friend.

But Twilight Sparkle suddenly felt worried. They might have the same hair and the same face and the same clothes and the same pet, but how could someone who had never had a friend or even had anyone to sit with at lunch possibly be like the Princess of Friendship? What did she know about friendship? Nothing. Absolutely nothing. Less than nothing. In fact, at the end of the Friendship Games, she had turned into the won stevous Midnight Sparkle.

Sunset Shimmer noticed that Twilight Sparkle was uncomfortable about something. "Are you okay?" she asked. "It can be hard being the new kid sometimes. Believe me, I know."

Twilight Sparkle smiled. Sunset Shimmer was so nice. All these Canterlot High girls were so friendly and forgiving. They hadn't blamed her or held a grudge about her opening the portal or anything.

But Twilight Sparkle wondered how to be a friend. What was she supposed to do? What if she turned into a monster again? It was all so confusing. If only someone could teach her what she needed to know.

Brand-New
Buddies

✶ ✶ ✶

Twilight Sparkle had been putting off returning to Crystal Prep to finish cleaning out her old locker. Her classmates there weren't very nice. One afternoon, when school was over, she took the bus over to Crystal Prep, hoping no one would be around.

She was putting some old pens and pencils in the front pocket of her backpack when she heard some giggling. She whirled around to see Sunny Flare, Sour Sweet, and Sugarcoat standing right behind her.

"Well, well, well." Sunny Flare smirked. "You're back. Giving up on your new school already?"

"I'm not," Twilight Sparkle protested. "I'm just picking up some last things."

"You don't want to forget a single homework assignment, do you?" sneered Sour Sweet.

Twilight Sparkle's cheeks flushed. She never knew what to say to these girls. "I've got to go. Bye," she said, hurrying down the hall. But her phone pinged, and she stopped to check it. It was Sunset Shimmer. *Do you know how to do the math homework? Want to come over and do it together?* she'd texted.

Twilight was just about to reply when Sugarcoat grabbed the phone out of her hand. "Ha!" she laughed, reading the message. "They already know that you're a brainiac."

"Here, dearie, let me help you," said Sunny Flare, her voice oozing sweetness. *Haven't started yet,* she typed back to Sunset Shimmer on Twilight Sparkle's phone. *Doing it later. Looks hard.*

Twilight Sparkle gulped. Were these girls right? Maybe she needed to make an effort to do things differently this time. After all, she was starting over at a new school.

"Don't be such an eager beaver," said

Sugarcoat bluntly. "Can't you just try to play it cool for once?"

When Twilight Sparkle was·at Crystal Prep, she had been an outcast because she liked to study. The other girls teased her because she asked questions and cared about what she was learning. But at Canterlot High, her new friends seemed to welcome her curiosity. At lunch, the girls asked her about her favorite classes, and it seemed like they cared. Maybe they were only pretending.

Ping! Sunny Flare looked at the text. She laughed. "Rainbow Dash is inviting you to go to the climbing wall with her."

"Could I please have my phone back?" asked Twilight Sparkle.

"Dearie, I'm going to give you back your phone, but I'm also going to give you a little advice."

"We all are," agreed Sour Sweet.

"We're just telling you these things because we're your friends," Sugarcoat added.

"But you're not my friends." Twilight Sparkle looked confused.

"We could have been. You just didn't know how to act right," Sour Sweet explained.

The other girls nodded in agreement. They clustered close to Twilight Sparkle, Sunny Flare still holding the phone.

"You've got to try to be cool for once," explained Sour Sweet.

"Yeah. Don't be such a goody-goody. Don't believe everything these girls tell you. They're sizing you up. They might drop you tomorrow," Sugarcoat warned.

Ping! Ping! Ping! All kinds of messages were coming in on Twilight's phone. Sunny

Flare glowered at them. She seemed upset. "Boy, they can't leave you alone, can they?" she said.

"Look," Sugarcoat ordered. "Pull out one of those pencils and write this down and study it, okay?"

Twilight Sparkle took a deep breath. "Okay."

The girls let loose with a series of recommendations as soon as she was ready.

"Don't trust anyone, and don't believe anything."

"For goodness' sake, hang back a little. Remember, they've all known one another a long time. You're the new girl."

"Just try to be cool, okay?"

"And find an ally!"

"An ally? What do you mean?" Oh, this all felt so confusing to Twilight Sparkle.

"An ally. The person you share the dirt with."

"The dirt?" Twilight Sparkle stopped writing.

"The gossip! You've got to gossip. That's how you team up with your best friend."

"Are a best friend and an ally the same thing?"

"Yes!" shouted all three girls together.

Sour Sweet giggled. "You're hopeless, aren't you?"

"I guess I am," Twilight Sparkle admitted.

The girls handed her back her phone, urging Twilight Sparkle to reach out to them for guidance.

"We're here for you!"

"Bye!"

"Bye!"

Twilight Sparkle heard them laughing as

she headed out the door. On the bus, she looked at her phone. There was a message from Fluttershy inviting her and Spike over to a special puppy spa, and another from Applejack wanting to plan a picnic. Twilight was so happy. She'd never been invited to do anything like that before.

She'd never realized what a difference friends could make until she came to Canterlot High. She loved how the girls waited for her at her locker and how they would catch up at lunchtime and save one another seats on the bus. But maybe there were more things that she should be doing as a friend.

She took out the list they had made her write and studied it.

Ping! It was another message. Pinkie Pie was having a slumber party. *Everybody in for tomorrow night?* she texted.

Yes! answered all the girls on the group message.

Twilight Sparkle answered with a thumbs-up symbol. It was so cute! She hoped it was the right thing to do. She had never used one before.

She looked down at her phone. Another message! Just for her. It was Sunset Shimmer.

Pick you up before the party? That way you don't have to show up by yourself. We can even get our homework done together before if you want.

You bet! answered Twilight Sparkle without thinking. Oops! Was that uncool? Oh, she was hopeless.

Twilight Sparkle thought of the time when she unleashed her magic at the end of the Friendship Games, sprouting wings and turning into Midnight Sparkle. She had become all-powerful but felt more alone than she had ever been before. Sunset Shimmer had rescued her from all of that. Sunset Shimmer had once made the same mistake, and the other girls had forgiven her.

Hey, she texted Sunset Shimmer. *Just let me know if I start to turn into a she-demon tomorrow night, okay?*

LOL! Sunset Shimmer texted back.

Twilight studied the text. It certainly seemed friendly. Was Sunset Shimmer a potential best friend, or rather, an ally?

She sighed. This friendship stuff was just so hard. If only it were as easy as math homework!

CHAPTER

2

Matching Mates

✸ ✸ ✸

Pinkie Pie had gone all out! She'd dipped balloons in glue and glitter, draped shiny streamers covered in silver stars across her bedroom ceiling, and decorated cupcakes with rainbow sprinkles. "This is a special celebration," she squealed when all the girls had arrived. "This is our first sleepover with Twilight Sparkle!"

"Yay!" screamed the girls together.

"Awww." Twilight Sparkle blushed. Sunset Shimmer squeezed her hand. They had put their sleeping bags next to each other on the floor of Pinkie Pie's room.

"It's great to have one together before Camp Everfree," said Rainbow Dash.

"Totally," agreed Rarity.

"What's Camp Everfree?" asked Twilight Sparkle.

Rainbow Dash smiled. "It's when we pack our overnight bags and go on a wilderness adventure together with camping and swimming and—"

"Marshmallows!" interrupted Pinkie Pie.

"And hiking and ghost stories and—"

"More marshmallows!" Pinkie Pie laughed.

"It's going to be like having a whole week of sleepovers together."

Twilight Sparkled gulped. She didn't have the heart to tell the girls this was her first sleepover. But at least she was going to have a lot of practice, thanks to Pinkie Pie and her parties.

Each of the girls had come with a special game to play. Rarity opened up a big cosmetics kit. It was filled with all different colors of nail polish—red-hot reds, shiny silvers, perfect pinks, wonderful whites, and even vivacious violets. Twilight Sparkle had never seen so many wonderful colors.

"Ooooh!" squealed Pinkie Pie. "I call pink for my toes."

"Not so fast." Rarity laughed. "In this game, we don't choose the colors; the colors choose *us*!"

"That doesn't make any sense at all," said Applejack, scratching her head.

"It does if you are playing Spin the Nail Polish!" Rarity announced.

"I love that game." Fluttershy clapped her hands.

"It's my fave!" agreed Rainbow Dash.

"Let's play," said Sunset Shimmer.

All the girls sat down in a circle on the floor. Twilight Sparkle was clearly confused, but she tried to play it cool. She didn't want the girls to know how out of the loop she was.

Luckily, Rarity filled her in. "When it's your turn, you pick a nail polish color and spin it in a circle on the floor. When it stops spinning, it will be pointing toward someone—and that person gets one nail painted that color. We don't stop until everyone's nails are done."

"It's like a magical makeover," said Pinkie Pie. "Kind of."

"You go first," said Fluttershy to Twilight Sparkle. "What color are you going to pick?"

Twilight looked at all the colors in the cosmetics box, but she couldn't decide. All of a sudden, she felt like it was a big deal and she might make some kind of mistake. Could you choose a wrong color? She took a big breath and picked a bottle of silver polish.

"*Oooh!*" Sunset Shimmer exclaimed. "I hope I get that color."

"Give it a good spin," suggested Rarity.

Twilight Sparkle twirled the bottle. It

spun 'round and 'round, finally stopping with its white top pointed at Applejack.

"Oh geez!" cried Applejack. "Now I'm going to look like one of the Dazzlings!"

"Are not!" said Rainbow Dash.

"Never." Fluttershy shook her head.

"Who are the Dazzlings?" asked Twilight, confused.

"It's a long story. Don't worry about it," said Rarity. "You just paint one of Applejack's nails."

"Okay," agreed Twilight. But she felt a little lost, a little left out. Had Applejack said that on purpose? She didn't think so, but she couldn't get the Crystal Prep girls' advice out of her head.

Sunset Shimmer noticed. "The Dazzlings were these girls who came here from Equestria to sow discord among us."

"But Sunset Shimmer stopped them!" said Applejack.

"Oh," said Twilight, trying to follow along as the girls chatted about Battles of the Bands and the lyrics to songs she had never heard of. She painted Applejack's left index fingernail very carefully.

"That's right pretty!" said Applejack admiringly.

"Thank you." Twilight Sparkle glowed inside. Maybe she was doing okay after all.

With lots of giggling, the girls spun their bottles of nail polish. Rainbow Dash, who wanted nails of every color, ended up with every finger painted red. Flutter-shy was happy with her hands a lively mixture of purples, golds, and reds. Pinkie Pie couldn't stop laughing when she ended up with green fingers. She waved her hands back and forth to dry them.

"I just hope you brought some nail polish remover!" said Applejack, looking at hers.

Rarity shook her head. "Oh no! I forgot!"

Everyone laughed some more. Twilight was having a blast. Her fingers alternated blue and white. She thought they looked beautiful.

"Hey," said Sunset Shimmer, noticing them. She held up her own hands. Her nails were also blue and white.

"Wow!"

"Cool!"

"Awesome!"

"How did that happen?" wondered Rarity.

Sunset Shimmer shrugged. "I don't know. The Magic of Friendship, I guess!"

The girls laughed, but Twilight Sparkle

was so happy. She and Sunset Shimmer matched! It was perfect.

"I love this game!" said Twilight Sparkle.

Rarity smiled at her. "Thank you, darling! I aim to please! Now, what's next?"

CHAPTER

3

Ready or Not, Here They Come!

★ ★ ★

"Sardines!" announced Rainbow Dash. "Who's hiding?"

"Me!"

"Me!"

"Me!"

The girls were all jumping up and down excitedly.

"This is my favorite game," whispered Fluttershy to Twilight Sparkle.

"I pick...you." Rainbow Dash pointed at Sunset Shimmer.

Twilight Sparkle was baffled. She had no idea what was happening. Sunset Shimmer got to her feet, left the room, and shut the door behind her. Pinkie Pie turned on some music, and the girls began chatting.

"How long should we give her to hide?" Applejack wondered.

"Five minutes at least," answered Rainbow Dash.

"It's best when she finds a really tricky place!"

"She will. I'm sure of it," said Fluttershy.

Twilight summoned her courage. "And what happens after she hides?" she asked.

The girls looked at her, amazed.

"You've never played sardines?" asked Rainbow Dash.

Twilight shook her head, a little embarrassed. Totally not cool.

"It's called sardines because everybody ends up all squished in someplace secret together, like those little smelly fish that come in a can all piled up on top of one another," babbled Pinkie Pie.

Twilight Sparkle's eyes were wide.

Rainbow Dash burst out laughing. "I can imagine why you wouldn't want to play that!"

"It's easy," said Fluttershy sweetly. "I like to think of it as playing baby squirrels hiding in a little nest in a tree. Except all the squirrels have to be very, very quiet so no one else will find them."

Twilight Sparkle was still confused.

"Let me explain the rules," Rainbow

Dash offered. She was the captain of some Canterlot High teams and knew exactly how to get everyone up to speed. "It's kind of the opposite of hide-and-seek. One person hides, but when you find her, you have to join her. One by one, we'll all pile in with her wherever she is."

"It's a blast!" said Rarity.

It did sound like fun to Twilight Sparkle. But she worried, too, about being left out. If the other girls found one another first, what would they do without her? She hoped that wouldn't happen.

"Okay," said Rainbow Dash after a few more seconds had passed. "I think that's enough time. Ready or not, here we come, Sunset Shimmer!" She flung open the door, and the girls dashed to all corners of the house, opening closets and looking under beds.

Twilight Sparkle stood in the upstairs hallway, thinking. Where would Sunset Shimmer hide? Somewhere tricky because she was so smart! Maybe she was behind the shower curtain in the bathtub. But she wasn't.

Rarity raced by her, giggling. "Sunset Shimmer found a good spot this time."

Maybe Sunset Shimmer was hiding under the stairs in the broom closet. Twilight waited for a moment when all the girls were somewhere else and opened the door a little tiny bit. She peeked inside. But there was just a vacuum cleaner and some cobwebs. No Sunset Shimmer. Where could she be?

Fluttershy was standing in the kitchen

looking around. "I guess she's not in here!" she said to Twilight Sparkle.

Maybe Sunset Shimmer waited until all the girls had left Pinkie Pie's bedroom and then snuck back in and hid under the bed. That's what Twilight Sparkle would have done. Twilight Sparkle raced back upstairs and checked. But Sunset Shimmer wasn't under the bed. No one was. Twilight listened carefully. She couldn't hear the other girls anymore. The whole house was very quiet. A clock ticked somewhere. Outside, the wind whistled.

"Hello?" called Twilight Sparkle. No one answered.

Twilight Sparkle searched from room to room. All the girls had disappeared. Everyone had found Sunset Shimmer—except for her. She tried not to feel disappointed.

She tried not to feel left out. It was just a game, wasn't it?

She heard a muffled giggle. Where was it coming from? She dashed toward the laundry room and noticed a big pile of dirty clothes. They were wiggling! The girls were underneath them. They had to be. She pulled away a towel.

"Surprise!" shouted the girls, tumbling out in a pile of laughs.

"We thought you'd never find us," said Applejack.

"Phew!" said Sunset Shimmer. "It was hot under there."

"That was the best hiding place ever," Rainbow Dash complimented her. She pulled some lint out of her hair.

"You were brave to burrow under all those dirty clothes," said Fluttershy.

"Sunset Shimmer's always brave," said Rarity. "Stealing crowns, battling Sirens—she jumps right in."

Happily chatting, the girls skipped to the kitchen for cider and cupcakes.

"I love cupcakes," said Applejack.

"I love frosting," said Rarity, giggling.

"I love sprinkles!" Pinkie Pie laughed. She had some on her nose.

Twilight Sparkle had been feeling a little down, but the moment she saw Pinkie Pie, she burst out laughing. She was so funny and so happy. Maybe slumber parties weren't so scary after all.

CHAPTER

4

The Pony Posse

★ ★ ★

Back in Pinkie Pie's bedroom, it was time to dance. Every girl had a favorite song and a special move.

"The way it works is you get to pick the music and the steps and the rest of us join in, as best we can!"

"No ballet moves, Rarity," begged Rainbow Dash.

"Just a few." She laughed.

Twilight Sparkle was worried that she wouldn't be able to keep up, but she loved the songs the other girls played. They had such good taste in music. She let herself go and be silly. She wiggled her hips and stomped her feet and waved her hands and tossed her head just like everyone else.

"You're a great dancer!" Fluttershy said.

"Love the way you lift your knees," agreed Rainbow Dash.

"Watch me!" said Pinkie Pie, going wild and making everybody fall to the ground with laughter.

Applejack changed the song to a country tune. "Look at me riding a bronco and busting a move!"

The girls imitated her, flipping their hands over their heads like they were swinging a lasso to catch a cow.

When it was Rarity's turn, she chose a catchy techno favorite. "Imagine you're on the runway," she instructed the other girls. "And show off your outfits!"

"You mean my pajamas?" Sunset Shimmer laughed.

Pinkie Pie put a pillowcase on her head. "Look how fashionable I am!"

Rainbow Dash challenged everyone to keep up with her fancy hip-hop steps. Fluttershy had them all strutting around to some pop music. Sunset Shimmer put on classic rock and roll, and the girls let loose. Twilight Sparkle was breathless from laughing so much.

She knew exactly what song she was going

to play when it was her turn. She had it all planned out. It was perfect. She got it ready and clicked play. It began with a steady beat like stomping feet. The girls all stopped, listening to the familiar intro. Was it? It was!

It was their band, the Sonic Rainbooms!

"Hey, hey, everybody, we're here to shout that the Magic of Friendship is what it's all about."

"Hooray!"

"Yay!"

The girls were thrilled. They tossed their hair and sang along.

"Great choice!"

"You're the best, Twilight Sparkle!"

Happily, the girls posted silly photos of one another, "liking" each and every one.

Later on, as they were getting ready to settle down, a message lit up Twilight Sparkle's phone. It was Sunny Flare!

Saw the photos. Cute.

Thx, answered Twilight Sparkle.

You would let someone post a photo of you making a face like that?

Uh-oh. Twilight Sparkle hadn't thought about that. Were the Canterlot High girls going to make fun of her dance moves tomorrow? No, they couldn't. She looked up from her phone, and Pinkie Pie grinned at her.

Another message came in. From Sour Sweet. *Bet your "friends" talked about things that happened before you came to Canterlot High.*

Twilight Sparkle gulped. *They filled me in on everything,* she protested.

Sure, they did, came the return message.

What did the girls say about you when you were out of the room? asked a text from Sugarcoat.

Twilight Sparkle was about to explain that she was never out of the room when she remembered the sardines game. But they hadn't been talking. At all. She would have heard them! Wouldn't she have? But maybe they had been whispering very, very softly.

Twilight Sparkle suddenly felt terrible. Tears welled up in her eyes. She shoved the phone into the bottom of her backpack.

"Everything all right?" asked the ever-sensitive Fluttershy, sensing Twilight's change in mood.

Twilight nodded. She didn't want to believe bad things about her new friends.

"This is my first sleepover," Twilight admitted.

Fluttershy wrapped an arm around her. "Oh!" she said. "We *all* get homesick sometimes, don't we, girls?"

"Don't you worry, darling," said Rarity. "I

once called my mother in the middle of the night to come get me."

Pinkie Pie snuggled close. "Confession: That's why I like to have the parties at *my* house."

"If you get a bad dream, you wake me up, promise?" Rainbow Dash ordered.

"Promise." Twilight Sparkle smiled. She didn't have the heart to tell the girls what was really worrying her.

But later on, when the lights were out, Pinkie had stopped giggling, and Applejack had stopped squirming in her sleeping bag, Twilight still couldn't sleep.

"What's the matter?" whispered Sunset Shimmer beside her.

Twilight Sparkle took a deep breath. "I don't know much about friendship," she admitted. It felt scary to open up about this and it was probably very uncool, but it was dark and it's always easier to talk in the dark. Besides, Sunset Shimmer was always so nice to her.

"Remember what Princess Twilight said," whispered Sunset Shimmer.

"What was that?"

"We learn about friendship from one another. It's something special, something magical that happens."

Twilight Sparkle wished she felt more confident. If only she knew more about friendship. She had never thought it was something she needed to study, but maybe it was. She had certainly learned enough about magic to open a portal to another world. Maybe she could learn enough about friendship to get what she had always wanted—her very own friends.

CHAPTER

5

Sixteen Signs You've Found Your Best Friend for Life

★ ★ ★

Twilight Sparkle hit the library the very next day. There weren't many books about friendship in the reference section, but every teen magazine she opened seemed to have an article, test, or list about it. She was carrying an armful to a study table when she saw the girls from Crystal Prep saunter into the library. They were always together in their tight little posse, chatting.

"Shh!" whispered the librarian.

Sunny Flare exhaled loudly, blowing her long bangs across her face. Sour Sweet made a little snorting noise. *"Hmmpf!"* said Sugarcoat with a toss of her long white-blond hair. The girls spotted Twilight Sparkle and made their way over to her table.

They slid into seats beside her and began flipping through the magazines.

"'Ten Ways to Identify Your BFF,'" read Sunny Flare.

"'How Do You Know When Someone's Really Your Friend?'" Sugarcoat pointed at the title of an article.

"'Besties Forever!'" Sour Sweet opened up to a headline in another magazine.

"Looks like someone is doing some research," observed Sunny Flare.

"Last night's slumber party not quite as successful as you'd hoped?" Sugarcoat's voice oozed with a nasty sweetness.

"I just wanted to…you know…make sure I was…you know…doing everything I could," stammered Twilight Sparkle nervously.

"Let's find out, then," said Sunny Flare, her eyes skimming over one of the articles.

"Here's a quiz," said Sugarcoat. "You're good at quizzes. Let's see if you pass this one."

Reluctantly, Twilight Sparkle answered the questions that Sugarcoat shot at her. But she hadn't done any of the things friends were supposed to do. She didn't make cookies. She didn't try different hairstyles. She didn't borrow clothes.

"But they have seen you at your worst!" Sour Sweet laughed. "That's the last question: *Do your friends still love you after seeing you at your worst?*"

"You sure were scary when you turned into Midnight Sparkle," remembered Sunny Flare.

Twilight Sparkle didn't feel very sparkly all of a sudden. What should she do?

"You should add these things to your list," said Sugarcoat. "You have the list we gave you, don't you?"

"Somewhere," said Twilight Sparkle.

"Invite Rainbow Dash over to make cookies," Sunny Flare suggested. "I'm sure she'd love that."

"And if she doesn't, then you know she's not your friend," added Sour Sweet.

Twilight Sparkle sighed. This was all so complicated. As the Crystal Prep girls wandered out of the library, she heard them bickering over whose house to go to.

"We always go to your house on the weekend," complained Sour Sweet.

"Maybe we should make cookies sometime. I love snickerdoodles," Sugarcoat said.

"Ew." Sunny Flare made a face. "Too sugary for me."

Twilight Sparkle picked up her phone and looked at the photos from the slumber party. Just seeing the happy, smiling faces made her feel better. Should she invite Rainbow Dash over to make cookies? Something just didn't feel right about that. She dashed off a text to Sunset Shimmer instead.

Hey! Do you want to come over and make cookies this afternoon?

Sure, came the immediate answer from Sunset Shimmer.

Twilight Sparkle sighed happily. This wasn't so hard. Not at all. It would be fun to share clothes and style each other's hair. They could do that, too. Maybe Sunset Shimmer wanted to borrow her purple boots.

When Sunset Shimmer arrived at Twilight Sparkle's house, however, she wasn't really that interested in baking chocolate chip cookies, which Twilight had already started. "We could just nibble on the chocolate chips," Sunset suggested. "That way we'd have more time to talk about magic. I want to find out everything you've learned. There's so much I still don't understand."

"You too?" said Twilight Sparkle, interested. "It won't take us that long to make the cookies, and while we stir the batter, we can talk."

"Okay," agreed Sunset Shimmer reluctantly. "Do you ever feel scared of how much magic you've got inside you?"

Twilight froze, a dollop of batter on her spoon. "What do you mean?"

"I told you what happened to me...." Sunset Shimmer expertly lined up a row of cookies on the tin. "But you clearly have special magic inside you. You sprouted wings and flew up into the air—"

"And got ready to destroy everything." Twilight sighed.

"Exactly," said Sunset Shimmer. "You don't want that to happen again, but..."

"I certainly don't," agreed Twilight Sparkle. "Hey, do you want to try on my purple boots?" she offered Sunset Shimmer.

"What?" Sunset Shimmer was confused.

"My boots. You can borrow them if you want."

"That's okay. I don't need to, but thanks."

Twilight Sparkle pursed her lips, thinking. "I have some fun hair ribbons if you ever want to wear one."

"Okay," said Sunset Shimmer. "Do you want to finish our homework together when the cookies are done?"

Twilight Sparkle bit her lip nervously. That was exactly what she wanted to do. But she didn't want to be a show-off. Still, maybe Sunset Shimmer would understand.

"Yes!" she agreed at last, but she added,

"We could braid each other's hair afterward, too."

Sunset Shimmer shrugged. "Rarity's better at that than I am actually. Maybe we should invite her over? And Applejack. She's great at baking...."

"Oh no!" Twilight Sparkle was alarmed. Was Sunset Shimmer bored? Did she want to be with someone else? What could she do to show Sunset Shimmer she could have a good time? "Here, let me take a photo of us both. Hold up your spoon!"

Spike bounded into the room. "Me too! Me too!" he barked.

Sunset Shimmer laughed and picked him up.

Twilight Sparkle showed Sunset Shimmer. "Do you like it?"

"Yeah, it's a great one of both of us."

Later that night, Twilight Sparkle made the photo her profile picture. Sunset Shimmer "liked" it a few minutes later.

Twilight picked up one of the cookies, nibbling on it happily. She and Sunset Shimmer were really becoming friends. They were!

I'm glad we're friends, she texted her.

Me too, answered Sunset Shimmer. And she included a little dancing-girl symbol with her message.

Twilight Sparkle pulled out her list and studied it. She checked off all the things she'd learned about in the library earlier. She wasn't doing that badly after all.

Her phone pinged. *Sunny Flare makes the worst cookies.* It was a message from Sour Sweet.

I'm sorry, Twilight Sparkle texted her back.

Yours looked better, came the answer.

You'll figure it out, answered Twilight Sparkle. *I'm sure you will.*

Twilight Sparkle felt like she had figured something out that day. It wasn't about baking cookies or taking pictures; it was something else, something a little magical, a little special. She had fun with Sunset Shimmer.

CHAPTER

6

Spike to the Rescue

★ ★ ★

Fluttershy was excited for Twilight Sparkle to come over with Spike. Because she was naturally quiet and a little shy, she always found it easier to get to know someone one-on-one.

She had everything she needed for a

very special pooch primp—doggy bubble bath, soft fluffy towels, a brand-new brush, and pretty clip-on bows. She'd even baked a batch of homemade dog biscuits. The puppies at the shelter really loved them. She hoped Spike did, too.

"Arf! Arf! Arf!"

Fluttershy could hear Spike as he came up the driveway with Twilight Sparkle. Long ago, when the Princess of Friendship first visited Canterlot High, Fluttershy became her first friend—all because of Spike. They both shared a love for animals. Fluttershy knew that Twilight Sparkle was her own person, and not necessarily *exactly* like the princess, but she had a feeling they were going to have a great time together.

Twilight Sparkle stopped in the driveway. She bent down to talk to Spike. "Remember,

Spike: Don't tell Fluttershy how I didn't have friends at Crystal Prep."

"But you did have a friend!" he barked. "You had me!"

"Oh, Spike," she said, nuzzling him. "You're the best. But remember, okay?"

She knew that she shouldn't feel nervous, but she did. She rang the doorbell.

Fluttershy skipped over to the front door to open it. Spike greeted her with a bark. Twilight Sparkle smiled and waved. She hoped that she would say all the right things and that Fluttershy would like her.

"I hope it isn't too much trouble having us over," said Twilight, coming into the house.

"Oh, no," said Fluttershy instantly. "I can't imagine anything I'd rather do. You ready for your makeover, Spike?"

"Yippee!" he barked. "By the way," he

added, "Twilight Sparkle was never unpopular at Crystal Prep. Just so you know."

"How could she be?" Fluttershy smiled.

Twilight Sparkle was embarrassed. She wanted to tell Spike not to bring up Crystal Prep again, but he was too busy enjoying Fluttershy's ear scratches.

"What a sweetheart!" Fluttershy said.

"He's my best friend," said Twilight.

"But not her only friend," added Spike. "Absolutely not."

Fluttershy smiled at Twilight Sparkle. "Of course not." She led them upstairs, where she had lit scented candles. The bathtub was filled with warm bubbles...and plastic chew toys.

"Hooray!" barked Spike, diving in. The girls laughed as he splashed them. He paddled back and forth in the tub.

"We need to give him a good scrub," Fluttershy explained to Twilight Sparkle. "Don't be scared of getting him wet."

"And I'm not scared of getting you two wet!" yipped Spike. He slapped his paws back and forth. The girls, covered in bubbles, screamed with laughter.

When Spike was all clean, they wrapped him up in towels and gave him a blow-dry. His purple hair got all fuzzy and staticky and stood straight up in the air. Twilight Sparkle grabbed her phone and began snapping photos of him. "Can you take a photo of me with him?" she asked Fluttershy.

"Sure thing!" Fluttershy answered. "You two are adorable."

"C'mon. You get in the photo, too!" urged Twilight Sparkle. She took the phone, and all three of them crowded in for a group shot.

They dusted Spike with powder. Fluttershy taught Twilight Sparkle how to trim his nails. "Maybe we should paint them blue and white, just like mine." Twilight Sparkle giggled.

"That's not so good for him," Fluttershy explained. "Dogs often chew on their paws. Let's give him a biscuit instead."

"I brought cookies for us to eat," volunteered Twilight Sparkle. "Chocolate chip!"

"My favorite," said Fluttershy.

"Sunset Shimmer and I made them together yesterday. We had so much fun."

"I hope you'll bring Spike to the shelter one day. He'd have fun meeting the dogs I take care of," said Fluttershy.

Twilight's eyes lit up. "That does sound special."

"It really is," said Fluttershy.

"And I can make dog friends!" said

Spike. "I didn't have any dog friends at Crystal Prep. Not one. But I wasn't alone. Because I had Twilight Sparkle!"

Twilight laughed. Spike was just about the sweetest dog in the whole world—and he smelled a lot better now, too. When she got home, she posted the photo of her and Spike and Fluttershy. It felt like she had a new friend. How had she done it with all of Spike's embarrassing mistakes? She wasn't really sure, but she had.

CHAPTER 7

Pairing up
★ ★ ★

Rainbow Dash arrived at the climbing center early. She wanted to get everything set up so she and Twilight Sparkle would have plenty of time to tackle the walls together. The girls had all agreed that it was easier to get to know someone new one-on-one, and

Rainbow Dash thought wall climbing was the best way of all to make friends.

You supported your partner, by holding on to a belay rope while they navigated footholds and handholds as they clambered to the top. It was fun. Rainbow Dash had everything ready—harnesses, helmets, climbing shoes, and energy bars for when they were done. It was going to be a great morning!

She was coiling a rope when three girls she didn't know very well came over to her. She realized she'd competed against them in the Friendship Games. They went to Crystal Prep.

"Hey," said Rainbow Dash, raising her hand in a friendly way.

"You're meeting Twilight Sparkle here, right?" asked Sunny Flare.

"I am!" answered Rainbow Dash. "You girls climbing today?"

Sour Sweet cleared her throat. "We'd love to join you because, you know, Twilight Sparkle. She's not exactly the best at sports."

"You don't have to be the best to have fun," said Rainbow Dash. "You just have to want to try."

"*Hmm,*" Sugarcoat considered. "I wouldn't want her to ruin the day for you. You know how she is."

Rainbow Dash looked confused. "No. I don't. What do you mean?"

The three girls tittered. "Oh, you know," said Sugarcoat.

Twilight Sparkle burst through the door at that moment. "I'm sorry I'm a little late," Twilight Sparkle apologized. "I was finishing up my homework."

Sunny Flare raised an eyebrow. "See?" she whispered to Rainbow Dash.

Hopeless, mouthed Sunny Flare to Sugar-coat.

But Rainbow Dash ignored the girls. "Why don't you climb first, Twilight Sparkle? I'll hold the belay rope. You can trust me!"

"I know I can. That's what friends do. They trust each other." Twilight Sparkle was beaming. How did she know that? She just did. She could feel it inside of her.

She saw the Crystal Prep girls a moment later. They were shaking their heads like she had said something stupid. It was true Twilight Sparkle hadn't thought about what she was saying, but she knew it was true. She just did.

She pulled on her helmet and buckled

her harness into the ropes. She grabbed on to the first handhold and hoisted herself up the wall.

Meanwhile, Sunny Flare was bickering with Sugarcoat and Sour Sweet. "I've always wanted to try out the climbing wall. I call firsties."

"Sorry, Sunny," said Sugarcoat. "I've paired up with Sour Sweet."

Sunny Flare scowled, watching the other girls start to have fun. "Here," she said. "I'll make a video of you all."

Twilight Sparkle was struggling, but Rainbow Dash reassured her every time she slipped. "Wow!" she said encouragingly. "I can't believe this is your first time climbing."

"Really?" called down Twilight Sparkle.

"Really!"

Sugarcoat glanced over at them and

stopped focusing on Sour Sweet. Her hands loosened on the rope, and Sour Sweet slipped. "Ouch!" she shouted. "Watch what you are doing!"

Sunny Flare tittered. "Ha! I've got it all on film. You should see how funny you look."

Rainbow Dash looked concerned. "Climbing is serious business. Trust is serious business," she said to Sugarcoat.

But Sugarcoat wasn't listening. "Hurry up!" she shouted at Sour Sweet. "It's my turn now."

Twilight Sparkle had reached the top. "I did it!" she exclaimed.

"I knew you would," said Rainbow Dash.

When she came down, Rainbow Dash took a turn on the wall. But the Crystal Prep girls were fighting with one another.

Sour Sweet stormed out of the building. Sunny Flare was uploading her video and laughing.

"Don't do that!" Sugarcoat gasped, reaching for the phone.

But Sunny Flare ignored her.

Later on, when they were taking a break for energy bars, Rainbow Dash asked Twilight a question. "That was a hard team to play on, wasn't it?"

"What team?" asked Twilight, confused. "I've never been on a team."

"Crystal Prep," Rainbow Dash explained. "Those girls don't know much about teamwork, do they?"

"Oh, that's not true," said Twilight. "They're much better at it than I am." Weren't they always together? Wasn't she always alone when she was at Crystal Prep?

"Give yourself some credit, girl," said Rainbow Dash. "I know who I want holding my belay rope, and it's you every time."

That night, Rainbow Dash called up Apple-jack. "Those Crystal Prep girls were not very nice today at the climbing wall."

"I don't think they were very nice to our Twilight at Crystal Prep."

"They just don't know much about friend-ship, do they?"

"But Twilight does."

"I'm not sure she knows she knows it, if you know what I mean," said Rainbow Dash. "Maybe we can help show her she knows way more about being a friend than she realizes."

"*Ooh!* I like that idea," Applejack exclaimed. "But how do we do that?"

"We'll think of something. I'm sure of it."

Later, Twilight Sparkle looked over the list the Crystal Prep girls had given her. Something was wrong with it, she realized. But what?

CHAPTER

8

Cheering Chums

★ ★ ★

The next morning, the marching band was playing. The cheerleaders were waving their pom-poms. The stands in Canterlot High's gymnasium were full. The basketball game was about to begin! Each team's players trotted on to the court.

"Go, Canterlot High!" squealed Pinkie

Pie, jumping up and down. Out of the corner of her eye, she saw Twilight Sparkle enter the gym. Twilight looked a little lost. She was scanning the bleachers. "Over here! Over here!" shouted Pinkie Pie.

Twilight made her way through the crowds of kids and climbed up toward Pinkie Pie. Pinkie Pie gave her a big hug. "I've got noisemakers and streamers and balloons for us to wave!" Pinkie Pie told her.

"Wow!" Twilight Sparkle was impressed. "You know how to support the team."

"I do," agreed Pinkie Pie. "Look at Flash Sentry. Isn't he cute?" She pointed at Canterlot High's star player.

Twilight Sparkle blushed. "He keeps waiting for me at my locker," she confided to Pinkie Pie.

"*Ooooooh!*" Pinkie exclaimed singsongily.

"What do you think it means?" Twilight Sparkle wondered out loud.

Pinkie Pie laughed. "I've seen the way he looks at you in class, and he likes you because he likes you. That's what I think it means."

"It's not just because I look like Princess Twilight?" That was one of Twilight's lurking fears—that these girls liked her only because she looked like their old friend. What would happen when they found out what she was *really* like? What if she turned into Midnight Sparkle again? Would they still like her?

On the court, the referee blew the whistle, and soon after, Flash Sentry took a shot. The ball flew into the basket. Twilight Sparkle and Pinkie Pie jumped to their feet, cheering. Twilight Sparkle noticed Sunset Shimmer had just shown up and called out to her, "Hey, Sunset, we're up here!"

The moment Sunset Shimmer sat down beside her, Pinkie Pie began telling her all about Flash Sentry. The girls giggled together.

"What are you talking about?" asked Twilight Sparkle over the roar of the crowd.

"Sunset Shimmer knows everything about Flash Sentry," said Pinkie Pie. "Because she went out with him a long time ago, and she thinks he likes you, too."

Sunset Shimmer nodded. "And not just because you look like Princess Twilight. I think he really likes *you*."

"That's what I said!" announced Pinkie Pie.

Canterlot High scored another basket, and Twilight Sparkle jumped up again. But Sunset Shimmer and Pinkie Pie didn't join her; they were too busy talking. Twilight felt a little left out. But did she have to? Maybe she shouldn't give in to her doubts. Maybe she had to trust the ropes, like she had with Rainbow Dash. Maybe she should just let herself have fun.

The next time a player made a basket, she not only jumped up, but she let out a shout and a silly cheer she made up on the spot. She wanted to root for her new school. *"Ice cream, ice cream, banana split! The Canterlot Wondercolts are a real big HIT!"*

Pinkie Pie's eyes widened. Her mouth dropped open.

Had Twilight Sparkle just made a fool of herself? Was she hopeless?

No.

With a delighted giggle, Pinkie Pie took up the cheer. *"Ice cream, ice cream, banana split! The Canterlot Wondercolts are a real big HIT!"*

Twilight joined in. Sunset joined in. Soon, everyone in the stands was chanting Twilight's new cheer.

"You are such a goof!" Pinkie Pie laughed.

Twilight's face fell. "I guess I'm not very cool," she admitted to Pinkie Pie.

"Cool? Me neither! I'm a hot-pink Pinkie Pie!"

Twilight joined in the laughter. It was hard not to when you were with Pinkie Pie. She was just so fun and enthusiastic. She made Twilight feel all bubbly inside. Or maybe it was sparkly?

Sunset Shimmer was beaming at her. "It's funny," she said. "You are different than Princess Twilight, but you share something magical with her, too. I can feel it."

"You can?" Twilight Sparkle felt pleased.

"Yes," said Sunset Shimmer. "I really can."

CHAPTER

9

Best Friends Forever

★ ★ ★

After the basketball game, everyone poured into the Sweet Shoppe for hot chocolate, ice cream, and smoothies. Kids were talking about Canterlot High's latest win. When the players showed up, including Flash Sentry, all the kids cheered. The place was bopping as kids sang along to DJ Pon-3's tunes and danced. Twilight Sparkle, Pinkie Pie, and Sunset Shimmer, their arms linked happily, walked up to the counter.

"What can I get for you?" Mrs. Cake asked Pinkie Pie. "The usual?"

"Yes, please! With extra sprinkles."

"I'll have the same." Twilight Sparkle smiled.

"Me too!" agreed Sunset Shimmer.

Mrs. Cake handed the girls giant hot chocolates with a mountain of whipped cream and chocolate sprinkles. They tried not to spill them as they crossed the room in search of seats.

"Hey, Sunset Shimmer!" Scootaloo called out.

"Hey," Sunset Shimmer answered. "I'll be right back," she explained to Twilight

Sparkle and Pinkie Pie. She went over to catch up with the other girl.

Twilight Sparkle sat in the booth, sipping her hot chocolate and watching the other kids hang out. Rarity and Fluttershy arrived and wanted to hear all the news about the game. Rainbow Dash and Applejack came in, ordered smoothies, and slipped into the booth. They'd already heard about Twilight Sparkle's great cheer. They started it up again, this time with a little change.

"Ice cream, ice cream, banana split! Twilight Sparkle is a real big HIT!"

Twilight Sparkle was both pleased and embarrassed. Here she was sitting in a booth, her friends all around her. This was what she had always dreamed about—and it was happening. She didn't know how, but it was. Maybe friendship really was magic after all.

"A certain blue-haired basketball player hasn't taken his eyes off of you!" whispered Rarity.

"Really?" Twilight Sparkle gasped, sneaking a peek at Flash Sentry.

"Really," Sunset Shimmer said, coming over and nodding. She took a sip of her hot chocolate. "*Ooh*, yummy!"

"It is," agreed Pinkie Pie. "Extra sprinkles are the best!"

"Agreed," said all the girls together.

At the height of her happiness, Twilight Sparkle noticed the Crystal Prep girls sitting at a corner table. Sunny Flare was scowling as she scanned the room. Sour Sweet was drumming her fingers like she was bored. Sugarcoat was absorbed in her phone. Twilight Sparkle had always thought they were friends—but she suddenly realized that they never seemed to be having any fun together.

Rainbow Dash was whispering something to Rarity. Rarity nodded her head, smiling. "We need a sleepover," she announced. "Tonight. My house. Get ready for the best spa party ever."

"Yay!" exclaimed Pinkie Pie.

"That sounds like a blast," said Sunset Shimmer.

"Doesn't it?" Fluttershy smiled.

"I can live through the primping." Rainbow Dash sighed. "As long as we can play some Flashlight Tag after we're done."

All the girls laughed. "Of course we will," said Rarity.

Twilight Sparkle glanced over at the other table. She had a feeling inside about the right thing to do. It was like the feeling she had when she made the cheer. "Can we invite the girls from Crystal Prep?" she asked.

The group stopped chattering and stared at her.

"I think they'd enjoy it," explained Twilight Sparkle. "I think they could use a little friendship magic." She glanced over at their table again.

"They could certainly use some polishing," muttered Rainbow Dash.

"That's right nice of you," said Applejack. "Thank you for thinking of them. Shall we call them over?"

"Yes," said Rarity. She looked a little

nervous but determined. She got up and walked over to the table with the Crystal Prep girls.

"I'll bring some cider to the party," volunteered Applejack.

"Count me in for flashlights," said Rainbow Dash.

"I can bring ingredients for special face creams," Fluttershy offered.

"And I'll bring a craft project," exclaimed Twilight Sparkle. "Glitter and beads and thread. Everything we need for friendship bracelets."

"That's a fabulous idea!" Pinkie Pie clapped her hands.

"They want to join us!" Rarity seemed surprised. She waved to the Crystal Prep girls, and they waved back.

"What a great idea," Sunset Shimmer whispered to Twilight Sparkle. "You have a gift for friendship. You're a natural, just like the princess."

"I just hope those girls know how to behave," Rainbow Dash muttered under her breath.

But Applejack heard her and nodded in agreement.

Hey!" barked a small voice from beside their booth. "What about me?"

It was Spike! In the excitement after the game, Twilight Sparkle had forgotten to go home and take him for his walk. But he had found her anyway. He nuzzled up against her leg.

"You can bring Spike to the spa sleepover," Rarity told her.

Twilight Sparkled picked him up. "I'm sorry, Spike," she whispered to him. "You forgive me?"

"Always," he said softly. "That's what friends are for."

CHAPTER

10

Pamper your Pals

★ ★ ★

Rarity bustled around her bedroom, turning it into a spa for her friends. She decorated with hanging ferns, pretty throw pillows, and scented candles. She hung gauzy scarves from the ceiling and floated slices of lemon in bowls of warm water. She found a CD of the ocean, with the sounds of waves coming in and going out over pebbles. It was all very calming.

She arranged a circle of low beach chairs around a small table fountain and put a rolled-up towel on each one. Soon the girls would arrive, and she was ready.

On one table, she had laid out barrettes, pins, headbands, clips, curlers, and ribbons. That was her hairstyle station. On the other table, she had a pumice stone, clippers, emery boards, bottles of polish, and pony decals that they could put on their nails when they were done.

The doorbell rang! The guests were arriving!

When Rarity opened the door, Rainbow Dash was standing there, her arms filled with flashlights. "Hey," she said. "I wanted to get the Flashlight Tag game all set up before everyone arrives. Moon's going to be out tonight, so it will be extra fun in your backyard. I am ready to run!"

The Crystal Prep girls arrived at the same time. Sunny Flare stared at the flashlights, an unhappy expression on her face. This was not what she had imagined for a spa sleepover. She wanted a relaxing night. "I don't want to play Flashlight Tag," she said bluntly.

Rainbow Dash's face fell. She was disappointed.

Sour Sweet seemed a little embarrassed. "Maybe we can use them as if we have a fashion show. We can light one another up as we strut on the runway. We can light up whoever looks prettiest," she explained.

"That's going to be me," said Sunny Flare with a toss of her head.

"Okay," said Rainbow Dash, alarmed. She exchanged a worried glance with Rarity as they led the Crystal Prep girls up to the bedroom.

Sunny Flare handed Rarity a foil-covered plate. "I made my extra-special chocolate-covered strawberries for tonight," she said.

Rainbow Dash lifted up the tinfoil. She picked out a strawberry and took a big bite out of it. "Delish!" she said

"Those are for later!" Sunny Flare scolded her.

"Oh!" Rainbow Dash was startled. She put it back on the plate.

"Don't do that. That's gross!" said Sugarcoat.

Sunny Flare glared at her. "Don't be mean, Sugarcoat."

"I wasn't any meaner than you were."

"Yes, you were."

"No, I wasn't."

Fluttershy peeked into the room. She was a little nervous because she'd heard the girls fighting. "I'm not late, am I?"

"It's not fashionable to be late anymore," snapped Sunny Flare.

Sour Sweet and Sugarcoat nodded in agreement, but they looked more uncomfortable than ever. They were sitting in beach chairs. Every now and then they whispered something to each other.

"Don't eat the strawberries," Rainbow Dash warned Fluttershy. "They're for later."

Why had Twilight Sparkle suggested they have a sleepover with these Crystal Prep girls anyway? She couldn't imagine. But if it was what Twilight Sparkle wanted, she would try to be a good sport. After all, Twilight was always a good sport about whatever *she* suggested.

Fluttershy sat down on the edge of the bed. She smiled at the girls. "Have you ever been to a spa sleepover?" she asked politely.

"Of course I have," responded Sunny Flare.

"No, you haven't," Sugarcoat contradicted. "We talked about it, remember? But we never did it."

"Maybe I didn't invite you the time I had one," said Sunny Flare.

Sugarcoat's face crinkled up as if she was going to cry.

"You didn't invite me, either?" asked Sour Sweet. "I didn't know you *had* any other friends."

Sunny Flare glared at her.

Fluttershy had no idea what to say. When her pets were in cranky moods, she didn't fuss with them. She realized how hard it was hanging out with girls you didn't really know. How brave Twilight Sparkle had been to come to Canterlot High. How easily she had made friends with them. If Twilight could do it, she could do it. She'd be brave like Twilight.

She began chatting about the new litter of puppies at the shelter.

Sugarcoat perked up. "Do you have any photos of them?"

"I do!" said Fluttershy. She pulled out her phone and opened her photo album.

"Aww!" cooed Sugarcoat.

Sunny Flare glared at her. "I didn't know you liked puppies."

"Everyone likes puppies," said Fluttershy.

Applejack, Sunset Shimmer, and Pinkie Pie arrived, talking and giggling.

"Girl, you have outdone yourself on the decorations," said Applejack, coming into the bedroom.

"Fountains! Ferns! Candles!" gushed Pinkie Pie. "Hooray, this is going to be the best spa party ever!"

"Whoa," said Sunny Flare. "*Someone's* got a lot of energy."

Sunset Shimmer's eyes narrowed. "*Someone* knows how to have fun."

Sour Sweet clapped.

"Don't eat the strawberries!" said Rainbow Dash, noticing Applejack's hand headed toward the plate.

"She can eat them if she wants to," decided Sunny Flare.

"But you didn't want me to eat them." Rainbow Dash was surprised.

"But now everyone's here," said Sunny Flare, rolling her eyes.

"No. They're not!" the Canterlot High girls shouted together.

"Twilight Sparkle still hasn't arrived," said Fluttershy.

"Oh, our bad," apologized Sugarcoat.

"That's right," added Sour Sweet, nodding her head.

"I wonder why she's late." Sunny Flare pursed her lips, thinking. "Has she turned into Midnight Sparkle again?"

No one said anything.

Whoosh! Whoosh! Whoosh! The only sound was the music of the ocean over the mini loudspeaker.

"Why would she?" asked Rarity at last.

"We all make mistakes," Sunset Shimmer explained.

Sunny Flare looked concerned. "I don't know. It's just that once someone's turned into a monster...well, you know. You can't help but wonder if it might not happen again. It's so...you know, brave of you to invite her to spend the night."

"Just because someone's turned into a monster once doesn't mean they are going to do it again," Sunset Shimmer protested. "I should know."

"That's right," chimed in Applejack.

The doorbell rang. It rang again. A dog barked.

"Hello," called a voice. "Anybody there?"

It was Twilight Sparkle.

CHAPTER

11

A Cranky Crew

★ ★ ★

"Hey, everyone," exclaimed Twilight, coming into the room with Spike. "I've got beads and gems and stickers and charms for friendship bracelets. They are going to look so great! So, what's the plan for tonight? What are we doing first?"

She looked around the room. She noticed the glum expressions on everyone's faces. What was the matter?

Fluttershy broke the silence. "I brought the ingredients for oatmeal masks...."

"Oatmeal masks?" Sunny Flare wrinkled her nose. "What are those?"

"You grind up oatmeal and dampen it with a little water and put it on your face to dry. It makes your skin all smooth and soft...when you wash it off...I guess....I give the puppies oatmeal baths some-times...." Her voice trailed off. She noticed the alarmed expressions on the faces of the Crystal Prep girls. "It was just an idea. We don't have to do it."

Spike sniffed at Sugarcoat, and she patted him on the head. He wagged his tail.

"How about we play Flashlight Tag

instead?" Rainbow Dash suggested. "I brought the flashlight.

"We are not playing Flashlight Tag!" Sunny Flare stomped her foot. "I came to a spa party. I thought we would have a fashion show."

"What will we wear?" Pinkie Pie wondered out loud. "I didn't bring my designer pjs." She giggled.

Sunny Flare snorted and glared at her.

"I think it's a great idea," said Applejack. "Don't make fun of Pinkie Pie."

"I didn't *say* anything," Sunny Flare protested, raising an eyebrow. She tried to catch the eye of Sour Sweet or Sugarcoat but they wouldn't look at her.

"You were being mean!" Sugarcoat said under her breath. "I could tell."

"I wasn't!" hissed Sunny Flare.

"Stop bickering!" Sour Sweet ordered.

"Can you stop them from fighting?" Fluttershy whispered to Sunset Shimmer. "After all, you stopped the Sirens when they were out of control, and Midnight Sparkle when she took over Twilight."

"I think these girls are worse," Sunset Shimmer whispered back to Fluttershy.

"My stomach doesn't feel right," admitted Applejack.

"My head hurts," said Rainbow Dash.

"I'm dizzy," explained Pinkie Pie.

Spike was growling.

Rarity just looked upset. After all the work she'd done decorating and everything.

Sugarcoat sighed. "This party needs some help."

"Right?" agreed Sour Sweet, glaring at Sunny Flare as if it were her fault.

Twilight felt terrible. She'd suggested inviting these girls. What could she do? Maybe if they all got busy, they would stop arguing. Without a word, Twilight began spreading out the craft materials she'd brought. There were all different colors of yarn, embroidery thread, and plastic twine. There were charms and beads and spangles.

"*Ooh!*" cooed Rarity. "Everything is so pretty!"

Sour Sweet couldn't believe it. "You bought all of this for us to use?"

Twilight nodded. "Let's make friendship bracelets for one another! I'll make one for you first. What's your favorite color?"

"Green," she said. "Can I make one for you?"

"Absolutely!" Twilight smiled.

The girls dove in and began creating

their bracelets—except for Sugarcoat. "I don't know which colors to choose," she admitted shyly

"The colors that you like best! Don't overthink it, just have fun," advised Pinkie Pie helpfully.

Sugarcoat looked at her wide-eyed. For a moment, she hesitated, and then she grabbed a mix of green and orange threads. "They *are* my favorite."

Applejack laughed. "And they're pretty, too!"

Suddenly, everyone was getting along, laughing and talking. No one was complaining of having a stomachache anymore. Somehow Twilight was able to change everything. She'd known just what to do to break the ice.

The only one who still seemed to be

unhappy was Sunny Flare. The more relaxed and chatty Sugarcoat and Sour Sweet were, the angrier she got. She put a few beads on a piece of plastic twine and handed it to Sugarcoat.

"Here," she said, scowling. "Because we're best friends, right?"

Sugarcoat gulped. "Thanks. But can't we all be friends?"

"Absolutely!" chimed in Twilight. "It's great to have a lot of friends. We can have friends who like to study or bake or play sports or go on picnics or…you get the idea!"

"Really?" Sunny Flare wasn't so sure.

"Maybe there's a friendship game we could play," Sugarcoat suggested.

"Oh, but there is!" said Sunny Flare.

"What?" said all the girls at once.

"What is it?"

"What are you thinking about?"

"Maybe it's not such a good idea…" Sunny Flare teased them.

"Just tell us!" Rainbow Dash was exasperated.

"There's one way to find out if everyone really is friends," explained Sunny Flare.

"C'mon," urged Applejack.

Sunny Flare took a deep breath. "I think it's time for us to play… Truth or Dare."

CHAPTER 12

Truth Trouble

✶ ✶ ✶

There was a hushed silence in the room. It wasn't one of the games the Canterlot High girls ever played together. They'd never needed to. They told one another everything. Didn't they?

They weren't even sure if they knew the rules.

"I think you are supposed to make cards...." began Rainbow Dash.

"I've heard," Rarity announced, "that you can ask anybody any question you want."

"Anything?" asked Fluttershy.

"You've never played?" The Crystal Prep girls were amazed.

The rest of the girls shook their heads.

Sunset Shimmer pulled out her phone. "Let me do a little research on the rules," she said.

Sunny Flare rolled her eyes.

"Oh, we know how to play," Sugarcoat said. "We always play."

"Sunny Flare makes us," added Sour Sweet.

Sunny Flare glared at her. "There are a lot of different ways to play," she announced.

"But the way we always play is that each person creates two cards. A *truth* card and a *dare* card."

"I *knew* you needed cards!" Rainbow Dash was pleased.

"On one we write a dare…" continued Sunny Flare.

"Like what?" asked Fluttershy in a small voice.

"I don't know," said Sunset Shimmer. "Something silly, right?"

"But not *too* silly, right?" Fluttershy looked worried.

"Absolutely not," agreed the girls from Canterlot High.

"It has to be scary enough that you might take a *truth* card," added Sunny Flare.

"One time," Sugarcoat blurted out, "I had to drink a spoonful of this yucky mix of ketchup and mayonnaise and pepper and soy sauce and orange juice...I never want to do that again. I'll pick a truth card every time."

"There are *truth* cards?" asked Apple-jack. "We don't just ask any ol' questions we want?"

"No," said Sunny Flare, irritated. "Two piles of cards, and each person can choose either a *truth* or *dare.*"

Sunny Flare went to her overnight bag and got pens. She tore out some paper from a notebook. "All right, everybody. Let's get creative. This is the chance to get the truth out there, to find out what you've always secretly wanted to know about one another."

"How is this a friendship game?" Rarity whispered to Pinkie Pie.

Twilight Sparkle was very upset. She

didn't know what to do. It had seemed like the right thing to invite the girls from Crystal Prep—but what if they were mean to her new friends? Had she just ruined everything? She didn't think investigating magic would cause any trouble—and it nearly destroyed the world. Was she about to destroy her new friendships?

With pursed lips and sidelong glances, the girls slowly wrote out their cards. They placed them face down in two different piles.

"So," said Sunny Flare when everyone was done, "now someone has to volunteer to go first."

But no one did. The room was silent.

"We need to do *eenie, meenie, miney, mo* or something. Or roll dice. Or something," said Pinkie Pie.

"That's not a bad idea," agreed Sugar-coat. "You got any dice, Rarity?"

Rarity reached under her bed for an old board game box, rummaged inside, and found a set. "You roll first," she said to Sunset Shimmer.

Sunset Shimmer shook the dice in her hand and let them go. Twelve. Phew! She would go last, but Rainbow Dash got a two. She was going first.

"How hard can this be?" Rainbow Dash said, her hand poised over the cards.

"Truth? Or dare?" Sunny Flare whispered.

"Truth for me," announced Rainbow Dash boldly. "I've got nothing to hide." But she still hadn't chosen a card.

"You've got to pick it up, read aloud the question, and answer it," said Sour Sweet.

Rainbow Dash cleared her throat. She grabbed a card, read it over quickly to herself, and gulped. "Can I change my mind? Can I do a dare instead?"

"*No!*" said all the Crystal Prep girls. "Read your question out loud."

She sighed. "My question is: *Name the one person in this room you would least like to be stuck with on a desert island.*"

"So what's your answer?" Sunny Flare asked.

"I hope it's not me," Pinkie Pie blurted out. "I mean, I'm sorry if it is. But you should remember I've come to every single one of your games and cheered. I'd have a lot of energy if you were stuck with me on a desert island. I'd make huts and build rescue fires. You know it, right?"

Rainbow Dash laughed despite herself.

Pinkie Pie always made her laugh. Each of the girls was special to her in a different way. Each of them would be wonderful to have on a desert island. Fluttershy would tame the local monkeys—that was for sure—and Rarity would figure out how to dress them all in banana leaves. She didn't like to leave anyone out. She didn't want say any of the Crystal Prep girls. She was just getting to know them—that would make them feel terrible. *Hmm,* she thought. What could she say? How could she keep from hurting anyone's feelings? Then it hit her.

Rainbow Dash grinned. "I know who I would least like to be stuck with on a desert island?"

"Who?" asked everyone together.

"Myself," she said.

"No fair," said Sunny Flare, pouting.

"It *is* fair," said Rainbow Dash. "I'd hate to be alone. I like to be with my friends."

"Good answer," said Applejack approvingly. "Oh. Well, I'll guess I'll have to tell the truth, too. I'm next." She grabbed a card. *"If you had to choose between Fluttershy and Rarity, who would you choose for a best friend?"*

Applejack gulped. This was a terrible question! Fluttershy was so sensitive that Applejack didn't want to hurt her. But she adored Rarity, and just because she didn't always share her enthusiasm for fashion didn't mean that they weren't friends.

"I don't know," she said.

"You have to answer the question," insisted Sunny Flare

"I don't want to." Applejack folded her arms.

"It's because I'm not your best friend, am

I?" Big tears were welling up in Fluttershy's eyes.

"No!" Applejack exclaimed.

"No, what?" whispered Fluttershy.

"Nope. I'm not answering and that's that."

"That's not how you play!" exclaimed Sunny Flare.

"It's how I'm playing," Applejack announced firmly.

Sunny Flare made a noise of disgust. "I guess it's my turn. I'm going to have to show you girls how to play this game. I'm taking a *dare* card"

Sunny Flare picked a card. She read the dare to herself. She read it again. She placed it down carefully behind her.

"I don't want to do this!" She sighed

dramatically. "I don't want to have to do this, but a dare is a dare."

Sunset Shimmer was studying her. Something didn't feel right. "What did it say?"

"I hate to have to do this..." began Sunny Flare.

"What? What?" asked the girls.

"It said *Do You Best Impression of...*" She paused. "*Midnight Sparkle!* Here goes!"

She stood up and held her arms over her head and opened her mouth as wide as she could. She rumpled up her hair. She crossed her eyes. She howled and bellowed.

Everyone froze.

It was awful. It was mean. Really mean.

Tears were welling up in Twilight Sparkle's eyes.

"Stop that right now," ordered Sunset Shimmer.

"You're ruining the party," said Sour Sweet.

"Why do you always have to do that?" Sugarcoat asked. "Why can't we just have fun for once? Why can't we just be nice to each other—like these girls?"

Sunny Flare had been laughing, but she stopped. No one thought she was funny.

Fluttershy had reached out and patted Twilight Sparkle on the back. Applejack was sitting beside her protectively.

Rarity cleared her throat. "Sunny Flare. This is my house and my spa party, and we are not playing games like this anymore. Maybe you should go home...."

"No!"

It was Twilight.

CHAPTER 13

You gotta Have Friends

★ ★ ★

"Sunny Flare, you don't have to be like this. You don't have to be mean. You can have friends if you want them," announced Twilight.

"What are you talking about?"

"I've been where you are. I've been a monster, too. I thought winning was more important than friends. But there's nothing more important than friends. Nothing in the whole world."

"I have friends," Sunny Flare protested.

"Kind of," admitted Sugarcoat.

"When you're nice," agreed Sour Sweet.

"I just wish we could have fun like these girls," Sugarcoat added.

Meanwhile, Sunset Shimmer had picked up the dare card. "I thought so," she announced. "It says *Do a stupid dance*. It doesn't say *Imitate Midnight Sparkle*. That was your own idea. You came up with that yourself."

"Twilight's the one who's a real monster. Not me," protested Sunny Flare.

"We can all turn into monsters sometimes," said Sunset Shimmer. "But the important thing is to know when you do."

"And there's something even more important than that." Twilight's voice fell to a hush. "We're all going to forgive you when you do. That's what these girls from Canterlot High have taught me. We all make mistakes some times."

"You'd forgive me? Really?" Sunny Flare couldn't believe it.

"I would," said Twilight Sparkle. "Just don't do it again, okay?"

"If Twilight forgives you," said Rarity. "We all do."

Sunny Flare looked around her at the smiling faces. Suddenly, she felt silly and a little embarrassed. "I'm sorry, everyone. Really. Maybe it would be more fun to give one another new hairstyles than play Truth or Dare."

No one disagreed with her.

The girls settled down to primp and fuss and have a silly pajama fashion show. They even played Flashlight Tag in the darkened living room. Everybody was finally having a good time.

Later on they decided to go back to their friendship bracelets. They made special ones for one another.

"Every bracelet is so different and pretty," said Fluttershy.

"Just like every friendship," said Twilight Sparkle.

Just as the evening was winding down and the girls were settling into their sleeping bags, Sunny Flare brought out what looked like a large shiny bracelet covered in jewels.

"What's that?"

"Is that for a giant?"

"Nope!" said Sunny Flare. "It's a crown I made. For Twilight Sparkle. For a long time, we've told her that she was no good at friendship, but that's not true. We weren't. We were terrible at friendship. She's the one who knows how to reach out and be brave and friendly. It's like she's a princess of friendship." She placed the crown on Twilight's head.

"Woof!" barked Spike. "Now you really are just like the princess!"

"What princess?" asked Sour Sweet.

"It's a long story!" said Rarity.

And they stayed up late into the night telling their new friends all about Equestria.

CHAPTER

14

Getting to Know You

★ ★ ★

Twilight Sparkle decided it was time for her to throw her own slumber party—so the girls could get to know one another even better. Her new friends. Her old friends, or rather, her new new friends. Sometimes it was still a little scary reaching out to the

Crystal Prep girls, but the more she did, the more they sought her help. She made sure to invite them all over to her house to get to know the Canterlot High crew one-on-one before her party.

Applejack came over the first afternoon with Sunny Flare. They blared country music while breaking eggs and peeling apples. They danced and were silly and made jokes—and they forgot about the cupcakes, which burned. Sunny Flare was very upset about it.

"It's okay to make mistakes," said Twilight Sparkle, laughing.

Sheepishly, Sunny Flare pulled out a little notebook and wrote down what she said.

Twilight Sparkle laughed again. "Put

that away, girl, and trust yourself. You don't need a list."

"No, no, no," agreed Applejack. "What we need is to make some more cupcakes!"

Pinkie Pie had offered to help out with decorations for the party, and the next day, Twilight Sparkle went over to her house with Sour Sweet. Under her bed, Pinkie Pie had boxes and boxes of streamers, balloons, decals, paper plates, stickers, markers, and posterboard. "What kind of theme shall we do for the party?" asked Pinkie Pie.

"It's a Friendship Star party," Twilight Sparkle reminded her.

"*Hmm,*" thought Pinkie Pie aloud. "We need to shine up our friendships, don't we? So we need shiny things."

Sour Sweet's eyes lit up. "Glitter and

metallic streamers and…" She jumped up and down, very excited. "And we need sparkles. Lots of sparkles. For Twilight Sparkle!"

Twilight Sparkle laughed. "Really? You won't have too much of me?"

"Never!" Sour Sweet announced. "Let's put sparkles on our nails, too, okay?"

"Yes!" agreed Twilight Sparkle.

"I'm not being too enthusiastic, am I?" worried Sour Sweet a moment later.

"Never," said Pinkie Pie.

The next day, Twilight Sparkle stopped at the Animal Rescue Center with Spike. She peeked in through the door. Fluttershy was surrounded by puppies and kittens— and Sugarcoat was there.

"Can we come in?" she asked.

"Of course!" answered Fluttershy. "I was

thinking we should teach Spike a new trick for the party!"

"That's a great idea," agreed Twilight Sparkle.

"It is!" agreed Spike.

"Sugarcoat is gifted with animals," she told Twilight Sparkle. "She's such a help!"

"Do you think she's telling me the truth?" whispered Sugarcoat to Twilight Sparkle nervously.

Twilight Sparkle laughed. A whole litter of kittens had fallen asleep in Sugarcoat's lap. "You can trust Fluttershy. You can trust your friends."

Just before bed, Twilight Sparkle texted Rarity. *Could you come over before the party and help me decide what to wear?*

Yes! came the immediate answer. *Would you like to borrow my purple shirt?*

Really?

Really!

Twilight Sparkle lay in bed that night, tired but happy. What a busy week she was having! She had so many friends to keep up with these days. It was so much easier and more fun to have a lot of friends—friends to bake with, friends to giggle with, friends who loved animals, friends who played sports, friends who knew how to make you look your best, and friends who had seen you at your worst. Like Sunset Shimmer.

Sunset Shimmer had taught the most important lesson about friendship of all— and that was forgiveness.

The next day, Twilight met Sunset Shimmer at the Sweet Shoppe. Twilight ordered two hot chocolates with whipped cream and extra sprinkles.

"My favorite! And extra sprinkles, too," said Sunset Shimmer, sitting down with her at a booth. "You remembered!" She took a sip of her hot chocolate and smiled. "This hot chocolate is perfect!"

"Thanks to the extra sprinkles," said Twilight Sparkle. "I have a favor to ask you."

"Anything," Sunset Shimmer said.

"I want to make a really special playlist for the party, and I want there to be songs each girl likes. Can you help me do that? You know them so well."

Sunset Shimmer grinned. "I would love to."

"Do you think I'm ready for the school trip to Camp Everfree?"

"You're more ready than anyone," said Sunset Shimmer.

"Sometimes I worry I might turn into Midnight Sparkle again someday...."

"Well, if you do, I'll let you know! And you'll let me know if I'm ever a crown-stealing she-demon. Deal?"

"Deal!"

CHAPTER 15

The Magic of Friendship

★ ★ ★

When the girls arrived at Twilight Sparkle's, the house was pitch-black and absolutely quiet. But the moment they rang the doorbell, a light flickered on. As they entered the living room, everything was shimmering and glimmering, thanks to Pinkie Pie's decorating talents. But there was one surprise even for her. On the ceiling were constellations of glowing stars.

"Hey," Pinkie Pie said first, pointing at a bright star in the center of the room, "that star has my name on it!"

"And that one's got mine!" Sour Sweet exclaimed.

One by one, the girls realized that each of their names was on a special star.

"Each of you has lit up my world," explained Twilight Sparkle. "Each of you is a star in my sky."

Fluttershy wiped away a tear.

Rarity wrapped Twilight Sparkle in a hug. "This is the most beautiful slumber party I've ever been to."

"Thanks." Twilight Sparkle blushed. "I hope it's the most fun, too!"

There was so much to do. They played Flashlight Tag, and afterward, they came inside, put on their pajamas, and giggled as they pretended to strut their fashions on the runway. They made their own pizzas, topping them with cheese and sauce and vegetables. For dessert, there were the cupcakes—the second batch—that Twilight Sparkle and Applejack and Sunny Flare had baked.

"Now it's time for a performance," announced Fluttershy.

Twilight Sparkle clicked on some music—and Spike bounded to the center of the room. He was going to dance! He tapped his feet and wiggled his tail and sang along to the song. He was adorable, absolutely adorable.

"Spike wins the dance competition."

Applejack laughed. "Now the rest of us need to join in!"

"I've got the perfect playlist," said Twilight Sparkle, beaming at Sunset Shimmer.

"This is my favorite song!" Rainbow Dash shouted, jumping up. "How did you know?"

Twilight Sparkle winked at Sunset Shimmer. "I had a little help from one of my friends."

The girls jammed to the music. They danced and danced. They pranced and pounced. Breathless, they laughed and giggled and sang along.

"Rainbow Rocks" began to play. Hearing the familiar beat, the girls clapped their hands delightedly.

"We used to fight with one another; that was before we discovered that when your friendship is real, you say what you feel!"

The girls lifted their knees, waved their hands, and stepped in time to the music.

Twilight Sparkle let loose. She didn't even know it. She wasn't thinking about anything. She was just listening to her friends sing along to the music and dancing because she was so happy. She was silly and happy, happier than she had ever been.

Maybe she really did know something about friendship after all.

epilogue

No One Gets Left Out

★ ★ ★

Twilight Sparkle was busier than she'd ever been. She was managing Rainbow Dash's soccer team, building a website for Rarity's fashions, and volunteering at the Animal Rescue Center with Fluttershy. She got together on the weekends with the Crystal Prep girls and went to bake-offs with

Applejack. She never missed a chance to share a giggle with Pinkie Pie. Most afternoons, she and Sunset Shimmer hit the library to do their homework together. Twilight Sparkle had so many friends.

One day, Trixie came up to her in the hallway at school. "You have more friends than anyone in this whole school! How do you do it? What's your secret?"

"I just have fun!" responded Twilight.

"Really?" asked Trixie.

"Really," said Twilight Sparkle. "We should hang out sometime. Do you want to?"

Trixie's eyes widened. "Really?"

"Really," said Twilight Sparkle. She skipped down the hall happily. She might not ever be the Princess of Friendship, but she didn't need to be. She just liked being a friend.

ReaD HoW TWiLiGHt
came to CanteRLot HiGH!

Turn the page for the beginning of
Equestria Girls: Friendship Games.

CHAPTER 1

A Whole New Ball Game

★ ★ ★

Sunset Shimmer dashed toward Canterlot High. Her red-gold hair wafted behind her like a pony's wavy mane. She was so excited! She glanced at her phone one more time. Could the news really be true?

She ran over to the statue of the Wondercolt. Rainbow Dash and Applejack were already there, and the other girls were seconds behind her. "I got your text, Rainbow Dash," Sunset Shimmer exclaimed breathlessly. "Did something come through the portal? Is Equestrian magic on the loose? Did Twilight come back with a problem that only we can solve?"

Pinkie Pie giggled. "Has a giant cake monster covered all the cakes in the world in cake?"

Rainbow Dash was surprised that all the girls had overreacted. What did they want? Another trio of evil Sirens to infiltrate their school and try to sow disharmony? She held up her guitar. The emergency was that she had broken a string—and she really wanted to practice some new songs for their band, the Sonic Rainbooms.

Sunset Shimmer wrinkled her forehead. "I don't understand."

"I was just telling Rainbow Dash here"—Applejack sighed—"that a broken guitar string doesn't really qualify as an emergency."

"It totally does!" Rainbow Dash couldn't believe that Applejack, who played the bass, didn't get it.

But no one did.

Rarity was put out. "Really, Rainbow Dash, I was in the middle of sewing a very complex appliqué on my latest frock."

"And I was just about to tuck in my pets at the shelter. Now we'll have to start stories all over again." Even gentle Fluttershy was annoyed.

Something just didn't seem right, but Sunset Shimmer couldn't figure out what it was. "Why would you send all of us an emergency text for a guitar string?"

Rainbow Dash whirled around and pointed at a trio of girls sitting on the school steps. Apple Bloom, Sweetie Belle, and Scootaloo were all looking at the Rainbooms expectantly.

"Fans!" explained Rainbow Dash. "I was going to show our fans some awesome guitar licks, but I kinda need all six strings to do that. Got any extra?"

Rarity rolled her eyes. Fluttershy shook her head. Pinkie Pie threw up her hands, and Applejack turned out her pockets. They were empty. But Sunset Shimmer was always prepared. She rummaged through her backpack and pulled out an extra set of strings for Rainbow Dash.

She handed them to her fellow guitar

player. "But I'm pretty sure the music rooms are locked now. It's the end of the day after all."

"No problem!" said Rainbow Dash. She restrung her guitar and gave it a triumphant strum. "The acoustics in the hallway are perfect for power chords. C'mon, let's go!"

"You coming, Sunset?" Applejack asked.

"I'll catch up in a bit," answered Sunset Shimmer.

The girls followed Rainbow Dash into the school while Sunset Shimmer looked up at the pony statue, disappointed. It was a portal to Equestria, but she had no idea when it would open again. She loved her new friends at Canterlot High, but sometimes she really missed Twilight Sparkle. When would they see her again?

Sunset Shimmer took out her magic

journal. When she wrote in it, Twilight Sparkle could read her letter in Equestria. Sunset Shimmer was so busy writing that she didn't pay any attention to the yellow bus rolling to a stop in front of the school. She didn't notice when the doors slid open and a dark-hooded figure slunk out and slipped between the shadows to the statue.

The shadowy figure removed an electronic device that began emitting high-pitched beeps. For a moment, Sunset Shimmer looked up. What was that? But it was probably just feedback from Rainbow Dash's guitar.

A needle spun wildly on the strange device and pointed directly at the Wondercolt statue.

Sunset Shimmer read over what she had written.

Dear Princess Twilight,

How's life treating you in Equestria? Any cool new magic spells? It's been pretty quiet here at CHS since the Battle of the Bands. We still pony up when we play music, which Rainbow Dash just loves to show off, but I still can't quite grasp what it's all about. I would love to hear what you think about it when you have a sec.

Your friend, Sunset Shimmer

Sunset Shimmer closed the journal and went to put it back in her backpack. But why was the Wondercolt glowing? Was the portal opening? How strange! That's when Sunset Shimmer saw the hooded figure slinking into the shadows. "Hey!" she called.

Startled, the figure pointed the strange device right at Sunset Shimmer—and it went wild, beeping and buzzing and glowing. The figure shoved the device into a pocket and took off running.

"Hey!" Sunset Shimmer shouted. "Wait! Stop!"

Sunset Shimmer raced after the hooded stranger, but the person managed to cross the street just as the light changed and traffic streamed across the road. A car honked its horn as Sunset Shimmer stepped from the curb. A bus pulled up. Sunset Shimmer saw the hooded figure peeking out from one of the windows. Too late!

"Who was that?" she wondered out loud. And what were they up to? Sunset Shimmer was worried—but she was also a little bit excited. Could a magic adventure be about to begin?

CHAPTER 2

The Name of the game

★ ★ ★

Once the bus was far away from Canterlot High, the girl pulled down her hood and shook free a mane of dark purple hair streaked with pink. It was Twilight Sparkle— the very girl who shared a name with the famous pony from Equestria. Unlike the Princess of Friendship, however, she wore glasses and she didn't seem to have a lot of friends. She was all by herself on the bus.

The bus pulled up in front of an ivy-covered brick building. A sign above the door said CRYSTAL PREP ACADEMY. Twilight hopped off the bus, bounded through the front door, and headed toward a science lab. She took her strange beeping device out of her pocket. She plugged it into an enormous computer. Lights flashed, the hard drive whirred, and the device started to glow. A printer spit out a long series of sheets. Twilight studied them carefully while a ball of light traveled from the device along a series of wires and cables to a small table in the middle of the lab.

On the table was a glass dome, and under the dome was another, smaller electronic device. It snapped open like an old-fashioned phone and sucked the ball of energy into itself.

Twilight checked off something on her clipboard, satisfied. It was working, whatever it was.

Twilight powered down the computer. She lifted the glass dome and removed the new device. Behind her was a bulletin board, and on the bulletin board were photos—of all the Equestria Girls.

SPARKLY SLEEPOVER SURPRISES

The Equestria Girls love slumber parties! They love the planning, the decorating, the baking, the dancing, the giggling, and the games. They want *you* to have a great time at your sleepovers, too, and that's why they've put together their favorite activities for you to play with your friends. Turn the pages to put the sparkle of friendship into your next sleepover.

PARTY PLANNING!

Twilight Sparkle lets each of her friends shine at her special sleepover. She wants Applejack to help with the baking, and Pinkie Pie with the decorations. Who are you going to invite to your slumber party—and in what special way will each person contribute?

Who is going to bring the snacks?

_____

Who is decorating?

_____

Who's in charge of the music?

_____

Who's organizing the games?

_____

Who's choosing the movie?

_____

Who is going to giggle all night long?!

_____

FRiENDSHiP BRACELETS

The Equestria Girls make friendship bracelets for one another—and now you can, too! Decorate each bracelet in your own special way for the Equestria Girls. What color will Pinkie Pie's be? What will you draw on Fluttershy's? Let your creativity go wild!

Rarity

Rainbow Dash

Sunset Shimmer

Twilight Sparkle

Pinkie Pie

Applejack

Fluttershy

YOUR FIRST SLEEPOVER

Twilight Sparkle is nervous when she spends
the night at Pinkie Pie's for the first time.
Will she know what the other girls are talking
about? Will she know how to play the games?
Will she be able to fall asleep when she's
not in her own bed?

What were you nervous about
at your first sleepover?

_____

_____

_____

_____

_____

_____

_____

Sunset Shimmer arrives with Twilight Sparkle at Pinkie Pie's. Rainbow Dash explains the games. Fluttershy lets her know that she felt nervous at her first slumber party. How would you help a friend who was feeling a little shy or scared about spending the night at your house?

_____

_____

_____

_____

_____

_____

_____

TRUTH OR DARE!

Oops…we're not playing *that* game right now.

TRUE OR FALSE

1. Sunny Flare was Twilight Sparkle's best friend at Crystal Prep.

2. In Equestria, Spike is not a dog…he's a dragon!

3. At the end of The Friendship Games, Twilight Sparkle turned into Midnight Sparkle.

4. Rainbow Dash loves fussing with fashions.

5. Fluttershy has a gift for working with animals.

6. Twilight Sparkle transferred to Canterlot High because she wanted to meet the Sirens.

7. Sunset Shimmer turned into a she-demon once, but the Equestria Girls forgave her.

8. The Princess of Friendship has never actually visited Canterlot High.

Answers

1. False. Twilight Sparkle didn't have any friends at Crystal Prep.

2. True. But both the dog and the dragon are able to talk.

3. True. She did! But she discovered that power was not as important as friendship.

4. False. Rainbow Dash is a jock. She'll put up with primping and decorating, but she is happiest outside and playing sports.

5. True. Fluttershy volunteers at the Animal Rescue Center, and she loves puppies, kittens, hamsters, and all animals.

6. False. The Sirens caused trouble at Canterlot High during Rainbow Rocks' Battle of the Bands. The Equestria Girls are the reason for Twilight Sparkle's transfer.

7. True. Just like Twilight Sparkle, Sunset Shimmer once got into trouble. In the first Equestria Girls movie she stole a magic crown from Equestria and became all-powerful until she was stopped by Princess Twilight.

8. False. Princess Twilight spent time at Canterlot High as a student—when she was trying to find the lost crown Sunset Shimmer had stolen.

SUNSET SHIMMER'S PARTY PLAYLIST

Sunset's an amazing singer, and because she's originally from Equestria, she also has unique taste in music! What kind of music do you like? Brainstorm some songs for the ultimate sleepover party playlist!

1 "Welcome to the Show"

2 _____

3 _____

4 _____

5 _____

6 _____

7 "My Past is Not Today"

8 _____

9 _____

10 _____

SUPER-SILLY SLEEPOVER FILL-IN!

It's time for you and your friends to rewrite Pinkie Pie's sleepover! Fill in the blanks with your own funny words and see what happens.

With lots of giggling, the girls spun their _____ *(noun)* of nail polish. Rainbow Dash ended up with _____ *(adjective)* _____ *(noun)* painted red. Fluttershy was _____ *(adjective)* with her _____—a _____ mixture of purples and *(noun)* *(adjective)* golds. Pinkie Pie couldn't stop _____ing when she *(verb)* ended up with _____ fingers. She _____ed *(adjective)* *(verb)* her hands back and forth to dry them.

"I just hope you brought some _____!" said *(noun)* Rainbow Dash, looking at hers.

Rarity shook her head. "Oh no! I forgot!"

Everyone _____ed some more. Twilight was *(verb)* having a blast. Her fingers alternated between blue and white. She thought they looked _____! *(adjective)*

WHAT IS YOUR EQUESTRIA GIRL NAME?

Are you Lemon Cream or Peppermint Flower? Yellow Jelly or Mocha Gingerbread? Take the initial of your first name to find the first word in your Equestria Girl name and then the initial of your last name to complete it! Find your name and draw a picture of what you look like!

A	Apple	J	Jelly	S	Sweetheart
B	Butterfly	K	Key Lime	T	Taffy
C	Cream	L	Lemon	U	Ultra
D	Daffodil	M	Mocha	V	Vanilla
E	Éclair	N	Neon	W	Willow
F	Flower	O	Orchid	X	Xena
G	Gingerbread	P	Peppermint	Y	Yellow
H	Honeysuckle	Q	Queenie	Z	Zippie
I	Icing	R	Raspberry		

Let the Party Begin!

Decoration Ideas from Pinkie Pie

Pinkie Pie loves to decorate and here are some of her tips for turning your bedroom into a super slumber-party palace!

1. Blow up balloons. Dip the ends into glue and then into glitter. Hang them from the ceiling to create a sparkling, star-filled sky!

2. Use sheets and fabric pinned to the walls and ceiling to turn your room into a tent…or a fairy bower.

3. Glow sticks and glow-in-the dark accessories invite everyone to turn out the lights and whisper their secrets to one another.

4. Paper streamers, scarves, and even old skirts and cloth can be thrown over chairs and desks to transform the room.

5. Don't forget the music! Ocean sounds, dance tunes, and even forest bird songs can all create different moods and atmospheres. Pick a theme and have fun.

6. Finally, fill you room with pillows—throw pillows, floor pillows, big pillows, little pillows, lots of pillows. How else are you going to get ready for a pillow fight?

Time to eat!

Applejack's Favorite Snacks

1. Apple muffins are a great substitute for cupcakes. You can even frost them with cream cheese!

2. Make your own pizzas. Prepare bowls with different kinds of toppings—cheese, veggies, meats—ahead of time.

3. Everyone loves roll-ups!

4. *Mmmmmm*. S'mores! All you need are graham crackers, chocolate bars, and *marshmallows*.

5. And remember it wouldn't be an Equestria Girls' party without cocoa with whipped cream and extra sprinkles.

Game Time!

Rarity and Rainbow Dash Review the Rules!

Rarity's Spin the Nail Polish Makeover

Begin with a lot of different colors of nail polish. Sit in a circle. One girl picks a bottle, lays it on its side, and spins it. Where will it stop? The girl it points at has to paint one of her nails

that color. Repeat until everyone's hands are completely painted.

Take photos of your manicures! Are they silly? Or pretty? Don't forget to have some nail polish remover on hand in case of accidents…or so you can start over and play again.

Rainbow Dash Loves Sardines

Sardines is the opposite of hide-and-seek. Only one person hides in the beginning. Everyone else waits in the bedroom—for about five minutes—and then opens the door and begins the hunt. If you know where your friend is hiding, don't let anyone else know. Then, when you are alone in the room, sneak in beside them—in the closet, under the bed, or under the laundry like Sunset Shimmer. It's going to get very crowded in there! How long will it take for everyone to find the hiding place?

The last person to find the sardines is the next person to hide.

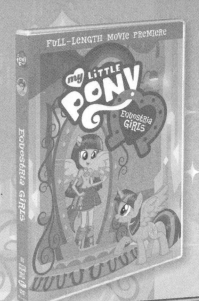

FULL-LENGTH MOVIE PREMIERE

ENJOY ALL THREE ADVENTURES

NOW ON DVD & BLU-RAY!